CW00833056

The Gollogans

in Winter

HELEN O'SULLIVAN

The Gollogans

in Winter

BOOK TWO OF THE GOLLOGANS SERIES

ILLUSTRATED BY DAVID HALLANGEN

WOODSORREL PRESS

Forthcoming by Helen O'Sullivan:

The Gollogans in Spring

The Gollogans in Summer

Other books by Helen O'Sullivan:

The Gollogans of Carrickgollogan

Language Learner Narrative

www.helenosullivan.ie

For Austin, Clara and Finn

WOODSORREL PRESS

Woodsorrel Press, Kilternan, Dublin, Ireland

This is a work of fiction. Names, characters, places, and incidents either are the product of the author's imagination or are used fictitiously. Any resemblance to actual persons, living or dead, events, or locales is entirely coincidental.

Copyright © Helen O'Sullivan, 2023

All rights reserved. Without limiting the rights under copyright reserved above, no part of this publication may be reproduced, stored or introduced into a retrieval system, or transmitted, in any form or by any means (electronic, mechanical, photocopying, recording or otherwise), without the prior written permission of the copyright owner and publisher of this book. For information, address: riverrunreadingroom@gmail.com

First paperback edition November 2023

Illustrated by David Hallangen
Book Design by Bea Reis Custodio

ISBN 978-1-7394210-3-8 (Paperback)

www.helenosullivan.ie

Contents

Chapter One
Autumn Festival

"Beware! Beware the pine marten!
With its long furry legs and its long
bushy tail,
We tried to save Harkin, to no avail.

Harkin looked to the left
And he looked to the right
And he twisted his body
With all his might!

But the pine marten pounced
And the pine marten ate
And the pine marten
Gollogans will
Never
Forget!"

With that the mamapapas closed in
a circle around the gollogeens. On cue
the gollogeens jumped up and screamed
and the mamapapas retreated. As part
of their autumn festival, the gollogans of
Carrickgollogan were all acting out the grim
scene of Mamapapa Harkin being preyed upon
by a pine marten. Despite the disruption of
moving to Knocksink, the show had to go
on. The autumn festival could not be missed
— the plays and stories conveyed important
wisdom and warnings to the younger
gollogans. Dil shifted closer to Indigo.

"What's up, Dil?" said Indigo.

"It's just, Harkin. I find it sad, that's all."

"Oh, I know. But it all happened a long
time ago. It's time for the story of Mamapapa
Plantain next! You love that one!"

Dil was upset that Indigo did not
understand how she felt, but Indigo was

right, Mamapapa Dandel told the very
best stories and Dil did love the story of
Mamapapa Plantain. She snuggled further
into her sock next to Indigo and saw that
Daffi, her yellow twin sister, and Bretia, a
young orange gollogan, had pulled a blanket
of moss over themselves.

Daffi knew she was meant to be feeling
drowsy and dozy and ready for the winter
sleep, but she did not. She felt restless and
impatient and excited, as always. It was even
worse now after she had spent days sleeping
off the effects of the giant drink she had
licked up in Carrickgollogan. Even after their
stay and all their antics at Evie and Jake's
house, Daffi was *still* full of energy.

Like Dil, Daffi was eagerly anticipating
the story of Mamapapa Plantain – the
gollogan who got away. Ever since they had
spent time in the Quinns' house, she had

been wondering about what it would be like to live in the giant world — *What was the rest of it like?* Daffi was just a little bit jealous that Indigo and Dil had got to stay at the Quinns' house first. She was supposed to be the adventurous twin!

Mamapapa Dandel stood in the centre of the circle of gollogans. "Are you sitting comfortably?" she asked. Gollogans and gollogeens all around nodded their heads. "Then I shall begin." She paused, taking in a deep breath and waiting for the right moment. The gollogeens were transfixed, their eyes only focused on Mamapapa Dandel. Mamapapa Dandel's own eyes scanned the room before settling on Daffi.

"Plantain lived many generations of gollogans ago, at a time when the giants still mostly rode on carts pulled by swishtails or walked on their own two legs. Great buildings puffed fumes into the air which could just be seen from Carrickgollogan Hill. The giants called these factories.

"One factory made a potion rather like our elderberry cordial, but it is said to be a heavy black drink. Giants called this factory the Great Brewery. Another factory made sweet crunchy snacks, the wrappers and remains of which we sometimes still find around the woods. These are what the giants call biscuits. In those days, as the city grew bigger below us, we had no worries about our homeland high in the woods. We lived peacefully and playfully, caring only to look after ourselves and our woodland friends. But Plantain was a restless gollogeen.

"Not content to settle in the woods for the rest of her days, she longed to explore the world. And so it was, that one day, Plantain got out to the road." Mamapapa

Dandel scanned the eager eyes of the gollogeens, before exclaiming: "And was seen!"

Dil gasped loudly and clung to Indigo.

Mamapapa Dandel continued: "Mamapapa Veronica, who had chased after her, was just in time to see Plantain picked up by a passing cart with colourful markings on the side. Mamapapa Veronica could not read it of course and so it was only much later that we found out what it was.

"The cart trundled away and Plantain was gone. The mamapapas ran out to the road every day in the hope that a passing cart might bring news or sighting of Plantain. Songs were composed to summon her back, but nothing more could be done.

"A week or two later a piece of paper found flying around the woods showed an astonishing picture of Plantain in the company of all manner of giants — one tall, one small and one with a beard all over its face. One, an extremely tall giant, had Plantain sitting on his shoulder. A gollogan in the care of giants? No one could fathom it. But she looked happy and well-fed." Dil relaxed her grip on Indigo and instead stroked her own tail, which she had flopped around in front of her for warmth. Her ears were fully alert as Mamapapa Dandel continued,

"But the mystery bothered the gollogans. What *had* happened to Plantain? The paper was kept for several gollogan generations until the letters on it were growing quite faded. That was when foolhardy Speedwell — your great-great grandfather, Daffi and Dil — chanced asking a passing boy giant if he could read it for him. And we learnt that the scribbles meant 'Travelling Freakshow' but we always regretted talking to that boy giant. The giants had found out about us."

Dil looked wide-eyed at Indigo, the tip of her tail now flicking anxiously.

"For many months they tried to trap and catch us up on the Carrickgollogan Hill," continued Mamapapa Dandel. "No doubt to put us in a freakshow or use us for other giant games. And that is when we had to escape down to the leadmines tunnels, our old home." With that Mamapapa Dandel paused and sighed. All the gollogans of Carrickgollogan sighed with her, remembering their homeland around the leadmines tunnels, recently devastated by forest fire.

"And now, here we find ourselves once again in a new homeland, thankful for the great generosity of our sinker gollogan cousins here in Knocksink."

A deep blue elder gollogan, Mamapapa Cerulean, stepped forward.

"May I propose a toast? To the great good health of gollogans of all colours in all places!"

"To gollogans!" they all cried, each sipping from their acorn cups of elderberry cordial and shifting down under their moss, feathers and socks for the big winter sleep. The past weeks had been quite exhausting and all the gollogans and gollogeens fell asleep quickly. Except for one.

While everyone settled to sleep, Daffi was wide awake. Quite apart from the sleep she had had earlier in the autumn, the sinker gollogans had only brewed enough cordial to settle themselves for hibernation. So when the gollogans of Carrickgollogan arrived, they had diluted it with water so there was enough for everyone. But the watered-down potion was not quite as powerful as usual. And Daffi had only drunk half of hers. Plus, the stories of autumn festival had not served as the warning Mamapapa Dandel had meant them to. If anything, they had reminded Daffi how trapped she sometimes felt in this gollogan world. When she had lived in Carrickgollogan, she had always imagined that Knocksink was a magical faraway kingdom, somewhere exciting! Something different! But it was more of the same. More cold, more damp, more foraging, more giant mess. Her mind was a bee-swarm of ideas.

Daffi remembered staying at Evie and Jake's house. Evie and Jake were the kind giant children who had helped them all move to Knocksink in their mam's car. The house had been warm and there was so much food! Maybe the gollogan leader Amaranthine was wrong, maybe it would not be so bad to be kept as a giant's pet. Evie and Jake's woofer, Chaser, just lay around all day, ate food served up to him and then was brought on walks in the woods. Okay, so he did have to wear a lead and do what the family told him, but for the sake of a warm bed, the flickering box they called television and all the food she could eat, wouldn't it be alright? And maybe she would have a bit more freedom. She was not a daft woofer. She was a clever little gollogan. She could make acorn pasta for a giant family, do sewing and mending *and* she was learning to tell stories! She could also chop up their rubbish for them. Would that be enough? Did giants even chop up their rubbish? Maybe they would find other giant jobs for her.

Daffi lay next to Bretia listening carefully. Being a gollogan she had superb hearing, so once she was sure that all around her were breathing the slow breaths of deep sleep, she turned to her companion.

"Bretia?" she whispered.

"Hmmph," said Bretia.

"Bretia, are you awake?"

"Hmmph, hmmph," said Bretia.

"Bretia?"

Bretia slowly opened her eyes. "What is it, Daffi? I'm trying to have my winter sleep!"

"I can't sleep," said Daffi. "I just keep thinking how nice it was back at Evie and Jake's. Do you think we could go back there?

Or to another giant family? Evie and Jake were so kind. I think we're wrong. I don't think all giants are bad. Maybe most of them are nice?"

That woke Bretia up. Daffi was onto something! They had always been told that giants were bad news, but the Quinns had been so nice. Bretia was getting a bit fed up too. She was known as the sensible gollogeen and being called sensible all the time made Bretia feel boring.

"What's your plan, Daffi?"

"I think we should go," said Daffi.

"Go?" said Bretia, feeling nervous and excited all at once. "Go where?"

"Go and find a giant family, ask if we can live with them? I don't know, really. But I know I don't want to stay here!"

"Me too," said Bretia.

"Really?" said Daffi.

"Yes. But you know, Monty would have to come with us. I'm not leaving my brother behind. He can make up our three." The grown-ups had a rule for the gollogeens; they must always go on adventures in threes, so that if anyone got hurt, one could run for help and another could stay and help the gollogeen who was hurt.

"Don't be silly, Bretia! If we go by ourselves we don't have to follow the mamapapas' rules!" As usual, Daffi just wanted to leap into action.

"Yes, but it is a good rule, isn't it? Or they wouldn't have made it."

"Ah, Bretia!" said Daffi. "Okay, then, let's wake up Monty."

"You want to go *now*?" said Bretia, suddenly feeling scared.

"When else did you think?"

"But Mamapapa Nettie will be having her baby soon ... I was looking forward to it."

"Sure, that won't be until spring. We can come back and visit. If we go now, the acorns will be at their freshest. Plus if we go to sleep, we'll have to try to wake ourselves up again."

"Of course," trembled Bretia. She took a deep breath and tried to imagine she was as strong as a beetle. "Okay, let's do this!"

It took the gollogeen girls another half an hour to wake up fun-loving Monty. He would open one eye, look at them, then roll over and snore.

"Monty!"

Roll, snore.

"Monty!"

Roll, snore.

"Monty!"

And so it went on, until finally Monty shook off the effects of the elderberry cordial (he had

had a bit more than his fair share) and woke up. Always on the look-out for new fun to be had, Monty agreed immediately to Daffi and Bretia's plan, before Daffi had a chance to finish explaining.

Daffi, Bretia and Monty stole their way to the acorn pile and each stuffed a couple into their belly pouches. They were not quite sure what they were planning, but they knew it was going to be an adventure.

Plantain had escaped to the world of the giants. Perhaps they could too.

Chapter Two
Missing the Gollogans

It was not just the gollogans who were thinking about their time with the "giants". Evie and Jake were also wondering about the gollogans.

"Mam, do you think if we went to Knocksink, we would see where they are living now?" Evie asked.

"The gollogans are having their winter sleep, aren't they? We wouldn't want to disturb them," said Mam.

"We wouldn't have to wake them up, we could just look for them."

"Why would we do that?"

"Oh, I don't know. It just feels now like we never met them at all. Like it was all a strange dream."

"It does a bit, doesn't it?" agreed Mam.

"But we did meet them, Evie!" said Jake. "Mam, can we see the video on your phone again?"

"Alright then," agreed Mam. "For the five hundred thousand four hundred and ninetieth time," she joked.

They sat on the sofa together and Mam hit play. There was one video of the gollogeens splayed on their bellies in a line on the sofa staring goggle-eyed at the television. Purple-mouthed Russet was hiccupping every ten seconds from a belly stuffed with blackberries.

Then there was a photo of Evie lying on the floor covered in gollogans.

There was another photo of all the gollogeens in the dolls' house – one in the bath, one licking out the remains of blackberry juice from inside the wardrobe, one lying in the bed and another sitting on the dolls' sofa "watching" a wooden television. The gollogans had really enjoyed the dolls' house, because it gave them a better idea of what their new world was all about. The gollogeens had particularly loved playing in it and would try to copy what they saw Evie, Jake and their mam doing.

Amaranthine, the gollogan tribe leader, had huffed and puffed when she saw the photograph of them in the dolls' house. "We are not dolls," she said and went back to sewing some ivy leaves Evie had stripped from the outside wall of the house. Amaranthine had wanted some leaves because she knew a bit of sewing would keep her in a good mood, especially while she had to suffer so many humiliations and indignities in the giants' house. She was used to managing everything herself and while she appreciated Evie and Jake's kindness, now, as she had exclaimed a bit too loudly to Mamapapa Dandel: "We are being treated like pets!"

The trickiest thing about having gollogans in the house was that sometimes, depending on the level of light, they could not be seen! More than once invisible gollogans foraging for blackberries had been caught out by Evie walking across the kitchen. There would be a scuffle and a yelp and Evie would quickly lift her foot in surprise and hear the grumblings of a disgruntled gollogan. This went on for several days until everyone realised that if the house was dimly lit, the gollogans could be seen. This was a complete revelation! The gollogans had never had control over their visibility before. Daytime was trickier. It was okay during sunset and sunrise but in bright daylight putting on a dim light did not work. In the end Mam resorted to closing the curtains to get the right level of glow into the room to make the gollogans visible.

"Curtains closed all day!" Mam had grumbled. "What will the neighbours think? But needs must, I suppose ..."

The last photo was of Dil and Indigo in Knocksink. Evie had taken it just before they all said goodbye. Evie had a framed copy of it hanging in her bedroom and every night she would look at it and whisper goodnight to them. She wondered if Dil and Indigo had found any socks in Knocksink. They had told her that socks were best for the winter sleep. It turned out that the giants' rubbish had its advantages sometimes.

"I love that photo!" Jake cried. It was one he had managed to catch of Daffi who was mid-flight from Chaser the dog to the living-room shelves.

Daffi had been so funny in the house. At first all the gollogans were afraid of Chaser, but they gradually grew braver. Daffi and

Monty even kept creeping up onto Chaser's back when he was asleep. Then the tickly feeling would wake Chaser up and he would spin around in frantic circles trying to see what it was he could feel on his fur.

One day Daffi and Monty invented a game called "dogapult". They would climb up onto Chaser as usual, then, once he was spinning, they would jump from Chaser's back onto a nearby piece of furniture to escape. Their favourite was to shoot off onto the highest shelf possible in the living room. Whoever reached the highest shelf was the winner.

Once, Daffi nearly knocked a vase down on top of Mam's head. So then Mam had to clear all the breakable things from all the shelves in the living area. "Gollogan-proofing" she called it. Protecting the house from gollogans. Amaranthine also made Daffi and Monty apologise. They wanted to make

Mam an acorn pancake, but apart from the fact that it would only have been the size of a one-cent coin and not hugely filling, it was poisonous for humans, and that was even before Mam had conceived the terrifying thought of gollogeens getting busy with a hot stove in her kitchen. Unsurprisingly, Mam politely said "no thanks", but told them she appreciated the suggestion.

"Daffi was nuts, wasn't she?" said Evie.

"Yes, but so was Monty! They were so bold!" said Jake. "Every time I opened the kitchen cupboard, I would see Monty trying to climb into the cereal box with Russet."

"And what were *you* doing in the kitchen cupboard?" said Mam. Jake just gave a sheepish half-smile and stayed quiet.

Evie cut in: "Oh, you're right! I forgot about that! But Russet wasn't being bold.

He was just hungry. No, not just hungry,
ravenous! A great big hunger-monster!"

"A gobbling goblin!" said Jake.

"A greedy gobbling goblin," said Evie.

"He was voracious, you mean," said Mam, joining in.

"What's that?" asked Evie.

"He had a big appetite – wanted a lot of food," said Mam.

"Oh, yes, that's it!" said Evie, "Russet was a hungry, ravenous, voracious greedy gobbling goblin."

"Not like anyone else I know," said Mam, winking at Jake.

"Ah, Mam. I have to grow!"

"You do, and before you're all grown up I'll have to cut a hole for your head in our ceiling!"

Evie was still in her own thoughts. "I wish we knew what they were doing now. Have they really all gone to sleep?"

"Do you remember the night that Russet and Monty tried to get the remote control car working?! Daffi was sitting on top and Monty and Russet were trying to work the controls, but couldn't quite figure out the lever so they kept ramming the car into the wall!" Jake said excitedly.

"How could I forget?" said Mam. "I thought we were being burgled!"

Evie broke in again. "I really can't imagine Daffi and Monty sleeping for a whole winter. They barely slept when they were here!"

"You're right, Evie. Hard to imagine those two resting. I never thought I would say this after all the chaos they caused, but I am missing the gollogans too," said Mam. "Let's go for a walk in Knocksink tomorrow. Maybe we'll see them, maybe we won't, but Chaser needs his walk anyway."

I bet we do see them, Mam!

Evie did not say this out loud, but, if thoughts could be loud, which it seems they could, she thought it loudly to herself. Evie did not know how she knew, but she just had a feeling. Gran called it her intuition. "Her in-chew-ish-on." Gran had pronounced it slowly for her. And now her intuition was telling Evie that she would see the gollogans the very next day. And she believed it.

Chapter Three
The Bumblebee

B y the time Bretia, Daffi and Monty had stocked their pouches with acorns, dawn was breaking over the Glencullen River. The air was so fresh and dewy that the gollogeens felt wide-awake and full of joyous hope for the future.

"What a beautiful day!" said Bretia, as the gollogeens stepped out from their sheltered spot in the wall by the bridge.

"Yes!" agreed Monty. "Where should we start?"

"Let's go up the steep bank," said Daffi. "I'm sure I heard a giant say there is a field at the top. Maybe there are houses there."

"What do we want houses for?" asked Monty. Daffi had not told him the full plan yet.

"To see if the giants will take us in, of course!" said Daffi impatiently, as if Monty should have known.

"Oh! Isn't that a bit of a mad plan?" said Monty. "I mean, Evie and Jake and their mam are nice, but Amaranthine and the other mamapapas are *always* warning us about giants. 'Don't talk to giants, don't go near their cars, don't let yourself be seen on nights of unmasking, don't this, don't that ...' can't we just go on an adventure ourselves without getting giants involved?"

"But how would we look after ourselves, Monty?!" asked Bretia. "The whole point is that we convince a giant or two to make us their pets and then we can have as much food as we want without foraging and run around having fun in their house. Like Chaser does!"

"Oh yeah!" Monty paused for a moment. "Actually, that's a brilliant idea!"

The three of them kept moving steadily over sticks and rustling through piles of fallen leaves, trying to find the bridge over the river. Monty stopped again,

"But why don't we just go back to Evie and Jake's house? Didn't Evie want to look after us?"

"She did," admitted Daffi, "but we don't know where she lives or even if we'll ever see her again, silly!"

"Oh, yeah, I suppose so. Pity! I was getting to like their funny breakfast. It beat that weird seedy stuff they got from the pet shop, anyway."

"I know!" said Bretia. "What *was* that?! I'm sure some of it was wood shavings."

Daffi laughed. "I think you're right! But Evie told me it was meant to be birdseed. You know, seeds for birds to eat."

"Birdseed! Is that what they call it? Sounds like you put it in the ground and birds grow out of it! Haha! Imagine that! Little birds growing out of the soil. Giants really can be so odd," laughed Bretia.

"I guess they can," said Daffi, feeling a little bit less sure of her plan now. "Anyway,

we'll find some less odd giants — I'm sure we will," she said trying to convince herself.

"We will," agreed Bretia. She flicked her orange tail up straight, feeling more determined now.

"Hope so," said Monty. His own orange tail was low. They were all quiet then as they thought again about what they were doing.

The sun had now risen and they had a clear view of the woodland. Any blackberries remaining on the brambles had turned brown. Green, red, purple, brown — the changing colour of the blackberries was one guide the gollogans had to the passing of time. Autumn was in its middle phase and would soon be giving way to winter. Rain had soaked into the soil, turning the once dusty mud paths into a boggy sludge. Leaves of all colours speckled the ground. The river, swollen with heavy showers of rain, whooshed noisily along nearby.

"Is that herb robert?" asked Bretia, pointing to a pink flower with its studded ruby stems, clusters of five-petals and feather-like leaves.

"Yes," said Daffi, "but hasn't it got another name? A smelly name?"

"Stinking Bob!" said Monty. It was his favourite flower name. "But it has loads of other names, I think."

"Stinking Bob!" Daffi giggled. "Sure it's not Stinking Monty?"

"Or maybe it was Stinking Daffi," said Monty mischievously.

"Ah, stop it, you two," said Bretia. "It's late to be flowering, isn't it?"

On hearing the question, Daffi calmed down quickly, keen to show that for once she knew a bit more than Bretia. "Oh, I don't know. But you're right, there is not much else flowering now. Most of the flowers have gone to seed," she said. "Mamapapa Dandel told me that is why we have to sleep over winter usually, because there is no food around. No fruit, no acorns left, nothing. That's why we need to get to a giant house as soon as we can."

Just then the threesome heard a buzzing sound.

"That's not..." said Bretia, turning, shocked.

"It is!" said Daffi.

"A bee!" said Monty.

They all leapt under a shrub to watch. Most of the insects were their friends, but they were a bit wary of bees.

"It's a queen bee. A young one," whispered Monty.

"She is definitely not meant to be out! Didn't Mamapapa Lavender tell us that at autumn festival? That some bees aren't overwintering because the weather is too warm? Do you think she thought it was spring-time already?" said Bretia.

"I would say so. It's not that cold, really, is it?" said Daffi.

"No. Mamapapa Dandel and the others don't know why, but sometimes autumn is a bit warm these days," said Bretia.

"And it's nearly winter now!" said Monty.

"Should we tell her? She might not know," said Bretia.

"I guess we can't give up being gollogans completely," said Daffi.

"It *is* our job to look after the woods," said Monty. "I'll do it."

"No, I'll do it," said Daffi.

"Just don't annoy her, Daffi! The last thing we need now is you being stung by a bee."

"I won't. I won't." Daffi did *not* like being fussed over.

Daffi emerged from under the shrub and tried to follow the bee as she buzzed from plant to plant, desperately looking for flowers. The bee was about a third of the size of Daffi. Large, furry and pretty scary looking with its big black eyes and black and orange fur.

"Hello!" called Daffi. "Hello!" and then she remembered. Like the ants, the bees could only sense vibrations. They did not have ears. But how to send sound vibrations while she was buzzing about?

Daffi decided to try and get in her line of sight. It was risky, but Daffi did not care. The bee just buzzed over her head to the green leaves behind her.

Strange, thought Daffi. *It is like she can't see me*. She went back to Monty and Bretia. "I can't get her to look at me!"

"Wait a minute!" said Bretia. "Bees can't see some colours as well as others. Let me remember." Bretia paused for a moment. "That's it! They prefer purple and blue. They can't see red, but they might see yellow and orange. We're all yellow and orange, but maybe it's too dark because of the shade. She probably prefers the clearer colours of the leaves."

"You're a genius, Bretia! How do you remember all this stuff?" cried Daffi. Bretia blushed.

"Okay," said Monty. "So we just have to pretend to be a purple flower."

"Are you quite mad, Monty? We don't want her landing on us!" said Daffi, being just a small bit sensible for once.

"Oh, yes. Good point." Monty thought for a moment. "How about we pick a herb robert flower, wave it about a bit and when she comes towards us we can throw it on the ground."

"Now, that's an idea!" said Daffi.

"Alright," said Bretia, feeling not a bit alright about this plan.

Moments later the three of them were nervously in position. They had a herb robert flower and were waiting patiently for the queen bee to zoom towards them.

"Bzzzzzzzz.......bzzzzzzzzz...... bzzzzzzzz......" To the gollogeens' small ears, the noise was loud enough to nearly rattle their bones. They each clung gently to a petal, spaced themselves around the flower and waved it up and down. If Evie and Jake had been there, they would have said it was a bit like the parachute game they had played in preschool.

As the gollogeens gently wafted the petals, the breeze rippled their fur. Soon their floral signal had attracted the attention of the bee: "Bzzzzzzzzzzzzzzzzzzzzzzzzzzzzzzzzzzzzzzzzz."

"She's coming!" called Daffi.

"Quick! Throw it!" cried Monty.

But they had not set out their plan quite carefully enough. Bretia, Daffi and Monty all tried to throw the flower in a different direction, tearing the petals off and leaving them scattered. "Oh no!" they all cried, but somehow, strangely, it had worked. The bee came in to land beside them.

Bretia stamped out a quick friendly greeting. It was always best to be friendly with bees. Daffi was grateful she had invited Bretia now. Bretia always paid the most attention when they were learning insect communication in the mornings with Mamapapa Cerulean, a sky-blue gollogan. Their other teacher was Mamapapa Cobalt. Cobalt taught them about plant-life, and did not put up with much of Daffi's messing.

The bee looked at them. She did not buzz, because bees do not talk by buzzing. (That was actually the sound of her wings beating or when she was shaking the flowers with her wings and belly to get the pollen.)

Bretia tried stamping out a simple message. "It's winter. Time to sleep. No flowers."

The queen bee stared at them, so she tried again to be sure: "It's winter. Time to sleep. No flowers." The queen bee just buzzed off and carried on from plant to plant.

"That was a bit rude, wasn't it?" said Monty.

"She is a queen bee," said Daffi. "Everyone knows they just do as they please."

"Daffi! Really!" said Bretia. Daffi was being ungollogan-like again. "Kindness is the best policy! I think she just didn't believe me or didn't understand. I'm afraid she is going to try and lay her eggs now. We'll just have to leave it. It's sad that they won't survive the winter."

"Ah, Bretia. Sorry," Daffi apologised. "You're right. It is sad, but there's nothing more we can do now." The queen bee had buzzed a long way from them by this point.

"Let's just get to the bank and get on with our quest."

The threesome carried on in silence for a time, sad that the whole bee colony would be lost. As Mamapapa Cobalt always said, gollogans could only do their best to preserve the woodlands and all the creatures that lived there. Sometimes their efforts would be in vain. This was the first time that Daffi, Monty and Bretia had experienced that for themselves.

As day turned to night, they settled down to sleep under a shrub at the edge of the path. Huddled together, they kept as warm as they could, but now cold, tired and disappointed at not getting the bee to listen, it was just as if a great dandelion clock of hope and adventure had had its seeds scattered to the four winds. Would the rest of their journey go the same way?

Chapter Four
The Walk with Chaser

"Wellies?" called Mam.

"Check!" replied Jake.

"Waterproof trousers?"

"Check!"

"Raincoats?"

"Check!"

"Dog lead?"

"Check!"

"Let's go!"

Evie, Jake and their mam scrambled into the car. They were halfway down the road, Evie babbling excitedly about maybe seeing the gollogans, when they realised that Chaser was not in the car.

"How is he not here?" cried Mam, "I put him in myself!"

"Maybe he jumped out the other side, Mam? Was the door open?"

"Aagh, you're right Jakey, I left the back door on that side open. Here we go again." She turned the car round.

They were soon back at the house with Chaser bundled into the boot this time. He would not stop barking, as he was not keen on car journeys. Mam just hoped he would not throw up. That would be the last straw! She was not sure how much longer she wanted to be in charge of this mad dog. Maybe she could find him a better home? One down the country where he would have space to run and another dog for company. Birds to chase and cows to bark at. She could imagine that making Chaser happy. But just the thought of giving him away was enough. She could never do it.

"Woof! Woof! Woof! Woof! Woof!"

"What is he barking at now, Evie?" asked Mam.

"It's another dog out for a walk."

Evie craned around in her seat, trying to watch the disappearing poodle for as long as possible.

"It was wearing a sparkly pink coat. And being pushed in a buggy."

"In a buggy? Are you sure?" asked Mam, incredulous.

"Yes, a dog buggy, I think. Can we get one, Mam, for Chaser?" Evie winked at Jake.

"A sparkly pink coat or a dog buggy?" asked Mam.

"Not a sparkly pink coat, Mam," said Jake. "Chaser's a boy!"

"So what if he's a boy, maybe he would like it!" said Mam.

"So are you getting one?" asked Jake confused.

"No. Definitely not. Chaser already has the perfectly useful furry coat he was born with. I am just saying, don't go imposing your ideas of ..." Mam paused. "Oh, I don't know what I am saying! I'm trying to drive and here you have me trying to decide what clothes a dog should or should not be allowed to choose for itself. As if a dog would choose to wear clothes in the first place!"

"But what about the dog buggy?" Evie said mischievously.

Mam was silent then. Evie knew what that meant. Then all Mam said was: "Maybe the dog was ill. Couldn't use its legs. Now, please, just let me concentrate on the road!"

Evie and Jake looked at each other and smiled. They loved confusing Mam with mad ideas. There had been a poodle, true enough, but the poodle had been walking on a lead. A black lead on a white poodle. That was all.

The rest of the journey was quiet, but Evie was bubbling with excitement inside. She could not stop thinking that today she was going to see all her gollogeen friends again. She sat there trying to remember all their names: Russet, the red boy; Monty and Bretia, the orange twins; Dil and Daffi, the yellow twins; Verdant, the green toddler; Gurrem with the broken leg; Indigo and baby Violet. Evie was a little scared of Amaranthine, their leader, even though Evie herself towered above her, Amaranthine had a fierce energy about her that was at least eighty times her size and Amaranthine *was* very suspicious of giants.

"We're here, Evie!" Jake stretched up in his seat to see further out of the window.

Evie snapped herself out of her dreaming. They were in Knocksink! Before she knew what she was thinking, the words slipped out. "I can't wait to see them!"

Mam had just parked. She turned round to Evie. "I know, Evie, love, but you have to remember that they are likely asleep now. How about we just enjoy the walk?"

"Okay." But the bubbles of excitement kept fizzing in her stomach all the same. Maybe if she wished hard enough, the gollogans would come out and see her.

"Can we paddle in the stream today, Mam?" said Jake. But he heard the answer before they even walked much further into the woods. The stream was rushing wildly over the rocks. It was not the burbling and comforting trickle of a gentle stream, it was like the roar of an aircraft taking off. Definitely no paddling today.

"Look at those leaves, Evie!" Mam was pointing to bright yellow leaves hanging from a tree. *Why did grown-ups get so excited about leaves and things that were everywhere*, wondered Evie. *Leaves were normal, weren't they?*

"What a bright yellow!"

Oh, that was it, the colour. Evie started to look more closely. They were particularly bright. As if someone had come along with some of the yellow paint from her paint box. They were almost shining. Autumn leaves were most often an orangey-brown colour. Sometimes reddish, sometimes brown, but shining yellow was so cheerful on this cold November day.

Evie started to notice more of the leaves. "What are those ones, Mam?" she pointed to some with curly edges, which were dotting the bridge.

"Oak leaves," replied Mam.

"Can you take a photo?" said Evie.

"Yes, of course." Mam took out her phone.

"I'd love bedroom wallpaper like that!" said Evie. "All dotted with oak leaves!"

"Now there's an idea!" said Mam. "Maybe you could collect a few and make a collage?"

Evie started to gather some of the oak leaves, but they were a bit slimy and kept breaking between her fingers. "Maybe I'll just take one and draw it myself at home."

"Good idea!"

"Do you think there will be any blackberries left?" said Jake.

"You're not thinking about your tummy *again*, are you?" teased Evie.

"No," said Jake, scowling at Evie. "I just like picking blackberries, that's all."

"Well, there might be one or two. How about we follow the path round and check the hedge?" said Mam.

Little did Evie, Jake and Mam know it, but in the gaps between the rocks, supporting the bridge they had just crossed over, were huddled all the sleeping gollogans. Well, not quite all. Mamapapa Dandel had not drunk enough cordial and now found herself wide awake and horrified to discover that Daffi, Bretia and Monty had disappeared!

Mamapapa Dandel thought it was still a dream at first. Gollogeens did not usually go off by themselves without telling a mamapapa. They knew how dangerous the woodland could be. Daffi was also one of

Mamapapa Dandel's belly gollogeens, which meant that Mamapapa Dandel had given birth to her. Mamapapa Dandel was very, very worried. Dil was still there, thankfully, but Mamapapa Dandel was surprised to see that Bretia had gone. Monty — maybe — he was always looking for fun, but Bretia? She was so good and sensible! Mamapapa Dandel thought as she looked around the crevice, stunned for several minutes, wishfully thinking that the gollogeens might appear before her eyes. They did not.

No need to panic, Mamapapa Dandel told herself. *No need to wake up the other mamapapas. I'll find them soon enough.*

Overnight the temperature had suddenly dropped and it was now bitterly cold outside the crevice. The body heat of all the gollogans inside the crevice had considerably warmed the air in there. Now Mamapapa Dandel was shivering. It was best to keep going, she thought. Maybe to the car park? She ran across the oak-leaf-strewn bridge and headed for the main path. Dandel went at such a pace that she soon felt much warmer. She sniffed around as she went and was sure she could detect the smell of Daffi, but there had been a quick shower of rain and it was hard to tell. She would follow it down the path all the same.

As the sun began to set over the woods, streaks of sunlight fell onto the path, lighting it here and there in a gentle glow. In other places, the path was completely shaded. It was all rather beautiful. Distracted by the beauty of the light, her worry about the gollogeens, and with her nose to the ground trying to catch the scent of Daffi, Mamapapa Dandel was totally unaware of the giants coming towards her. And the woofer with them. She was also completely unaware that every time she headed into the brief glow of sunlight she could be seen.

"Mam! Mam! Look!" cried Jake.

Chaser pulled forward on the lead. Mam had learnt her lesson and never let him off now.

"Chaser, stop!" cried Mam.

"It's Mamapapa Dandel, Mam! It is! It really is!"

Evie ran ahead to say hello. "Oh! She's gone again! No, wait, there she is! Now she's gone again! Mamapapa Dandel! It's us! Evie and Jake!"

Mamapapa Dandel took fright at all the noise they were making and ran in under a shrub at the side of the path. After a moment, she realised how silly she was being and crept out again. Like Dil, she could be nervous at times.

"Oh! Evie and Jake, I am so glad to see you!"

"We're so glad to see you too, Mamapapa Dandel!" said Evie. "Except, right now, we can't see you. You're just a voice. Do you think you could move into a patch of sunlight?"

"Oh, yes, of course," Dandel braved, moving further onto the path into the low glow of the sun.

"That's better," said Evie, smiling. "How is everyone?"

"Evie, I need your help," said Mamapapa Dandel abruptly. "I'm afraid Daffi, Monty and Bretia are," Dandel hesitated, not wanting to say it. "Missing!"

"Missing?" said Jake. "How?"

"Get back, Chaser!" Mam had joined them now with Chaser and he was trying to push his nose up against Mamapapa Dandel, who ran in again under the shrub.

"Chaser!" Mam pulled him back. Evie peered under the shrub trying to see where Dandel had gone, but she had disappeared in the shadows. She put her hand down and called gently, "Mamapapa Dandel! Here! Climb onto my hand. You can sit on my shoulder."

The next second Evie felt the tickling sensation of a gollogan running over her hand, up her arm and onto her shoulder. Evie stood up again. Chaser knew better than to jump up on Evie. That was one thing he *had* been trained not to do.

"You'll be safe there, Mamapapa Dandel." It felt funny having an invisible gollogan on her shoulder, being able to feel her, but not see her.

"Thank you, Evie. Can you please help me find Daffi and Monty and Bretia? I am so worried about them! Your two long legs will be quicker than my four short ones. I think they went up the path that way."

"How did they go missing?" asked Jake.

"Well, I just woke up early from my winter sleep and they were gone!" said Mamapapa Dandel. "I hope an animal didn't find them in the crevice." She looked worried. "No, that can't be right, because they were sleeping at the back of the crevice. If anything came in, it would have found Dil and Indigo first."

"Here, Chaser, this way!" They all headed back into the woods, Chaser now pulling Mam back the way they had come. Now it was Chaser with his nose to the ground and he seemed very sure of which way he wanted to go. Mam was not happy about being dragged along by the "infernal dog," but maybe this time he was onto something.

"Why don't we follow Chaser?" suggested Jake. "He is a terrier! Aren't they meant to be good at finding small ... erm ... creatures?"

"Great idea, Jake!" said Mam.

"We'll find them, Mamapapa Dandel. I'm sure we will."

Determined, they all set off into the fading light of the woodland.

Chapter Five

Mudbath and Mountain Climb

Still slightly under the effects of the cordial, Bretia, Monty and Daffi had slept much longer than they had planned, and it was not until the afternoon of the following day that they continued on their path.

In fact, just a couple of hours before Evie, Jake and Mam met a worried Mamapapa

Dandel, Daffi, Bretia and Monty had turned left to go along the main path. They had kept in to the ferns and the ivy along the edge, so they could hide quickly if a woofer came along. Or a giant, of course. But woofers could smell gollogans, and sometimes see them.

They were looking for the perfect spot to climb the steep bank as the path they were on was quite boggy. The heavy showers had soaked the soil and heavy wellies had churned up great cliffs of mud surrounded by puddles of water. Daffi's plan was to reach the houses at the top of the bank, instead of stowing away in a car in the car park. That way, they could just go directly to their prize — a warm giant house.

"I'm so cold," complained Daffi, despite her fur. "Isn't it much colder than yesterday?" Little did they know, but

Amaranthine, in her wisdom, had timed the winter sleep perfectly. Daffi, of course, was rarely in the mood to heed wisdom. In all the excitement to leave straight away, Daffi, being her wild do-first-think-later self had not brought an ivy leaf tabard or even a bird feather cape for that matter.

"It is," said Bretia and Monty together. Everyone was feeling the cold. Bretia and Monty had not thought of bringing clothes either, but then, cautiously leaving decisions to Daffi, Bretia had thought the plan was to travel light, just with acorns to weigh them down.

A sudden squelch.

"Help! I'm stuck! I'm sinking!" Daffi had strayed into the boggy mud of a puddle. Bretia and Monty each grabbed one of her hands and heaved. And heaved. And heaved. Then suddenly: "Pop!"

Daffi tumbled out of the mud on top of Bretia and Monty.

"Ah, Daffi! Yuck!" cried Monty. "You've covered us all in mud!"

"No worries!" said Daffi. "We can just wash it off in the river!"

"Are you out of your mind?" said Bretia as if the question even needed asking. "Have you seen the river?" Bretia thought of the sticks and leaves she had seen spinning and skipping wildly over the rocks close to the surface, being bumped and tossed at great speed down the river. She did not want to go anywhere near the water herself.

"No, Daffi!" said Monty. "Mamapapa Cobalt warned us about that just last week. The river is so fast now after the heavy rains. We would all be washed away. You'll just have to stay like that."

"Yuck," was all Daffi said, feeling a bit sorry for herself. They continued silently up the path, more careful to avoid puddles. After a while the mud had dried, clumping Daffi's fur.

"Hey guys! I'm not cold anymore! I think the mud is keeping me warm."

"It's not keeping *me* warm," moaned Monty.

"Yes, but you've only got a little bit on you. I've got a thick coat of mud. Try it!"

Monty was shivering. So was Bretia.

"This had better not be a joke," said Monty.

"No joke. I promise," Daffi assured him.

Monty and Bretia soon found another puddle and carefully scooped up handfuls of brown gloop with their hands to plaster over each other. It felt slimy, wet and cold but somehow refreshing. Soon they were all three like little balls of melted chocolate apart from two eyes peeping out. Daffi was right. They did feel warmer. Then a sudden noise.

"What are *they*?!" called a voice. It was a young giant, pointing down the path towards them. He was no more than five years old.

"Quick, Daffi!" cried Bretia. "We've been seen!"

"Oh no!" cried Daffi. None of them had thought about the mud making them visible. Disaster! They ran in under the ivy.

"I can't see anything," called the older giant.

"There! They ran in there!" The young giant was squatting by their hiding place now, big eyes staring into the dark under the shrubbery. The gollogans closed their eyes tight. They did not want to frighten themselves with the sight of strange big giant eyes gawking in at them, but also hoped that with eyes closed they would be completely camouflaged against the mud around them. It worked. Then to their relief, they heard the young giant being called away.

"Come out from all that mud!"

"Oh, I can't see them now, Mammy."

"You and your imagination!"

The giants walked on.

Bretia's heart felt ready to leap out of her chest in terror.

"Are you sure this is a good idea, Daffi?"

"Of course not," said Daffi, taking things lightly. "Did I say it was a good idea? It's an adventure, isn't it?"

Bretia felt suddenly very tired again. She longed to be huddled in the crevice with the other gollogeens, bedding down for their winter sleep.

Daffi saw the look on Bretia's face. She did not need her friend giving up on her.

"Look, tell you what — let's stop here for an acorn. We need a break."

"Good idea," said Monty.

After munching their acorns in the shadow of some ferns, Bretia's eyes were closing. She had slept so badly the night before, shivering with cold and with fear. Soon she was gone. Monty and Daffi stared for a while at the flickering of Bretia's eyelids. They were starting to feel tired themselves.

"Should we wake her up?" said Monty at last.

"We have to get to a giant's house," said Daffi. "We have to find one before moonshine."

"Can't we just sleep here?" said Monty.

"It's too cold," said Daffi.

"Of course," said Monty. "I hadn't thought of that."

"Bretia!" Monty and Daffi shouted together.

And again, "Bretia!"

"Oh! What is it?"

"You were asleep, Bretia," said Daffi.

"Was I?"

"Yes, but only for two minutes," said Monty.

"I was having a lovely dream ... there was the fire and a cup of elderberry cordial. Then I was rock-hopping with Indigo and Dil and I was flying through the air off the biggest rock, then we were throwing sticks into the stream watching them drift away, faster and faster and ..."

"Really?" said Daffi. "You were only asleep for a minute. We have to get on and get to a giant's house before it gets dark." And just like that, Bretia was brought back to the cold, the descending dark and the company of Monty and Daffi on their mad adventure.

Gloom was gathering in the woodland as the afternoon wore on. The sun, which had lit up the bright yellow leaves earlier in the day, had disappeared.

The three gollogeens, only slightly refreshed by their acorns and caked completely in mud, now found themselves at the bottom of the steep bank. They had found their spot. At this particular spot there were tree roots cascading down out of the soil, ready for the sticky pads of gollogan hands and feet to cling onto.

The soil itself was soft, like play-dough, and soaked through. It was studded with grit in places, in others it was covered with a scattering of tan-brown leaves. These were very hard for the gollogans to grip onto.

"Here goes!" said Daffi.

"Here goes!" echoed Bretia weakly.

"Let's do it!" said Monty eagerly. The climb looked like fun.

But it turned out climbing the tree roots was hard work. The leaves and gritty soil were very hard to get a grip on and the grit soon coated all the stickiness on their paws. Scrambling up as much as they could, they would find themselves very often sliding back down. Being small and on all fours, it was never too fast, but the feeling of falling was still quite scary. Bretia thought her stomach would jump clean out of her mouth.

The easiest was when they found a clear stretch of fallen tree trunk they could get some kind of a grip on and scramble up the bank that way. It was incredibly steep. Far steeper than they had imagined when looking up from the bottom. And the deceptively easy climb at the beginning had fooled them. They came to rest behind a tree growing out of the bank. It was the only safe place they could rest without fear of falling. Here, they dared to look back the way they had come. It was like looking down a sheer cliff.

"I guess we just have to keep going up," said Monty with as much brightness as he could muster despite his fear.

"Yes," said Bretia.

"Of course," said Daffi, full of bravado. "There's no going back now!"

Bretia's arms and legs were beginning to tremble. But it was no longer from cold now. The coating of mud and the steep climb had warmed her up no end. The trembling was from the extreme effort of using so many muscles to haul herself up and up. And then from the fear of falling back down. She could feel her throat all tight and dry and her breath shallow. She did not want to say it, but knew the others knew. She was quite terrified.

"Are you okay, Bretia?" asked Daffi.

"Yes, yes, of course," said Bretia, not wanting to betray herself.

Monty knew his sister. He was not fooled. "Of course you're not, you mean! This is terrifying! In a fun kind of a way, I mean. Thrilling! Exhilarating!" Monty did not know it, but if he had been a giant he would have compared it to a rollercoaster ride. But rollercoaster rides are controlled and safe. This was not. This was real. That did not matter to Monty. He loved risky ventures.

"We're nearly there now anyway," he said.

"Are we?" Bretia finally dared to look up from the bank. She had been coping with the climb by staring only at the small patch of ground in front of her.

"Yes. Look!" said Monty. And so they were. Just ahead of them was a wire fence.

"That must be it!" said Daffi excitedly. The field! She had heard giants down in Knocksink talking about the field. The sinker gollogans had told her about it as well. At the top of the bank was a field and across the field were some houses. "We're nearly there!"

Chapter Six
The Giants

After a few short minutes of climbing, they were at the fence. The fence had been designed to keep giants out. But there was no way it could have kept Daffi, Monty and Bretia out. They easily slipped underneath and into some high grass. Swishing through it, they emerged on a path that ran around to one of the houses. But what they had not planned for was the enormous swishtail in the field near the house. They would have to get past it in order to get to their goal.

"Not something else! I think I've had enough adventure for one day."

"Don't give up now, Bretia!" Monty encouraged.

"Sure, you've no choice anyway. We're here now," said Daffi, boldly heading on and barely looking to see if the others were following her. "That swishtail won't care about us anyway. Not without its giant telling it what to do."

Daffi was right. The horse completely ignored them all and they made their way to the building. Outside was a faded slide with cracking plastic, a few bins and a few neglected pot plants, dry and withered.

"So what do we do now?" asked Bretia.

"Well, I suppose we knock on the door," said Daffi. "Isn't that what people did when they went to Evie and Jake's house?"

"Yes, but they were other giants. We're gollogans. We can't just turn up, knock on the door and say 'please keep us as your pets'," reasoned Monty.

Daffi looked at him. Why had she not thought of that? Or rather, why had she kind of thought that doing that would be okay in the first place? Now they had reached the destination, she realised that she had no decent plan at all. Inside she was thinking "*oh no*", but all she said to Monty was: "Well, do you have a different idea?"

"Well," said Bretia, "I might have an idea. Do you remember that book that Evie read to us?" The gollogeens had loved listening to the giants' stories. They were so different from the ones told by the mamapapas. "I think it was called, 'The Elves and the Shoemaker', wasn't it?"

"Oh, yes! I remember that one!" said Daffi. "I remember thinking that the little elves in the shoemaker's house were a bit like us being in Evie's house."

"That's it!" said Bretia. "That's the plan!"

"What's the plan?" said Daffi.

"What?" said Monty. Neither of them had cottoned on.

"We sneak into the house and do some helpful jobs around the place, then once the giants finally see us, they will be ever so grateful, like the shoemaker and his wife, and they might let us live with them!"

"Brilliant, Bretia!" said Daffi. "That was kind of my plan too, but," and this was a rare thing for Daffi to admit, "I hadn't quite thought it through."

"Well, at least now we have a plan," said Monty, trying to be kind.

Getting into the house turned out to be much easier than expected. In fact, it was much easier than when Dil and Indigo had turned up at Evie and Jake's house. The back door was already open. The three gollogeens ran in and hid themselves under a low shelf stacked with shoes. Across from the shelf they could see five pairs of wellies caked in mud: Green, black, red, orange and blue wellies. They could hear a television in the next room.

"Ooh, they've got a television," whispered Monty.

"Sssh!" said Daffi and Bretia together.

The door they had come in through led into a kitchen. From where they were, they could see all kinds of rubbish on the kitchen floor — breadcrumbs, a hair elastic, pieces of plastic building toys, scraps of paper, a bit of plastic food wrapper and a button among other things. Upstairs they could hear the noise of children's voices and feet thumping on floorboards.

"Maybe we could start by cleaning the floor?" said Bretia.

"Definitely needs it!" said Daffi.

"Yuck," said Monty. "Is that a half-eaten apple?"

"And a banana peel!" said Bretia.

"Helping out in this house does not look like much fun," moaned Monty.

"Maybe not," agreed Daffi, "but you wait until we are sleeping on warm beds and getting served all our meals. Then the fun starts!" Daffi was still daydreaming about being a giant's pet.

The gollogeens could not see up onto the kitchen counters, but if they could have, they would have seen tomatoey pans piled in the sink, coffee grounds and bits of pasta dried onto the kitchen worktop, a teetering pile of dishes waiting to go into a dishwasher already full of dirty dishes and a black cat on the prowl, up on the counter about to wee in the half-open cutlery drawer.

"Down, Smudge!" came a loud voice.

The cat leapt down, landing deftly on all fours.

"A scratchclaw," whispered Monty. Bretia and Daffi just stared.

Smudge started padding in their direction, dropped down to look under the shoe rack and miaowed. Quickly, a paw swiped in under the shelf. The quivering bundle of gollogeens huddled deeper into a corner.

Smudge kept miaowing and tried again.

An angry voice this time: "Shut up, Smudge!" Footsteps were coming in their direction.

"What if the giant sees us?" said Bretia.

"They don't sound too friendly," said Daffi, now feeling nervous herself.

"Not at all," said Monty. "Let's just leave, guys. We can go back out the way we came in. Try a different house maybe."

"Yes, let's try a different house," agreed Daffi.

"Out you go!" said the voice loudly.

Daffi was scared now, her sense of adventure long gone. "Other giants must be friendly like Evie and Jake and their Mam. Mustn't they?"

The cat disappeared from their sight and all they heard was the back door being firmly closed next to them. The giant walked back towards the television.

"They closed the door!" said Bretia. "What will we do now?"

"We have to find another way out," said Monty. "What else can we do?"

"Well," said Daffi, "in Evie and Jake's house the front door was opposite the back door at the other end of the house. Maybe we can just sneak across the kitchen, past the television and out the front door."

"Why would the front door be open?" said Monty.

"Oh," said Daffi. "I didn't think of that. How about an open window then?"

"In winter sleep time?" said Bretia. "I wouldn't say they have any windows open when it's *this* cold!"

Just then, they heard a bing-bong sound. It was the front door! Daffi recognised the sound from Evie and Jake's house.

"Quick!" said Daffi. "They have to open the front door now!"

Before Bretia and Monty could say anything, Daffi had shot across the kitchen. She paused on the threshold of the living room. As Bretia and Monty joined her they could see the back of a giant heading towards the front door.

"Now!" called Daffi. "While their back is turned!" They all set off as fast as possible across the living area.

"Ah, flip it. Mary! We've mice again!"

Another voice. There was someone else in the house! The gollogeens panicked. In the fading light, they could be seen! There was no furniture to run under and the huge man-giant was coming towards them. They froze. The delivery man had gone now and Mary turned round quickly without closing the front door.

"Where? Quick! Get them! Where's the broom?"

"The handle broke off last year, remember?" laughed the man-giant. "We never got around to getting a new one."

Bretia, Monty and Daffi stood stock-still. They were petrified and had no idea which way to go.

"Hang on a minute," said the man-giant. "They're some funny looking mice. What *are* they?"

"You're right there," said Mary. "Get that box over there, Mick!"

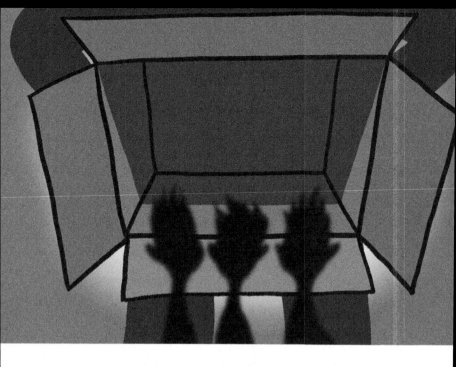

Within seconds Mick was looming over
them with a cardboard box about to land it on
top of them. The sight of it prompted them
all into action again and they raced out the
open front door into a sudden downpour of
rain. Daffi zipped ahead of Bretia and Monty,
who were breathlessly chasing her, mud
sliding from their fur as they went. Never had
Bretia been so terrified in all her life. Why on
earth had she decided that being sensible was

not a good thing? Daffi and all her mad ideas! And Bretia had dragged her brother into this crazed plan as well.

Bretia and Monty could no longer see Daffi, but they could smell her. She had zipped off towards the top of the steep bank. They too arrived at the top of the steep bank just in time to see Daffi carelessly diving forwards down the steep slope, landing some way down and then sliding on the gritty soil and leaves, flipping over and over in an unplanned series of somersaults, bumping her into tree roots and branches until she was out of their sight.

Chapter Seven
The Discovery

"**M**y toes are freezing!" complained Evie. "Mine too," said Jake.

"Oh dear," said Mam. "Jump up and down on the spot for a bit. Here Dandel, you hop onto my shoulder."

"Oh, no thank you," said Dandel eyeing up Chaser at the end of the lead as she leapt directly from Evie's shoulder to the ground. It was no bother to her as she was used to jumping far greater distances.

The gollogeens still had many years' practice ahead of them before they could leap like Mamapapa Dandel. Unlike most young animals, the gollogeens were a bit like humans in that they had to learn a lot of things as they grew instead of just being able to do them soon after being born. That was why they had gollogeen school, except that they did not call it school, but "drinking from the fountain", meaning the fountain of knowledge. Every morning the gollogeens would drink at the fountain.

After Evie had tried to warm up her toes, she picked up Dandel again and put her back on her shoulder. Everyone was getting cold and the daylight was fading fast.

"We're nearly back at the car park," said Mam. "I'm sorry Mamapapa Dandel, but I really will have to bring Evie and Jake home then. It's nearly their bedtime."

"Oh dear," said Mamapapa Dandel. "Of course. You can't stay here in the cold. Would you come back tomorrow?"

"Of course!" said Mam. "We will come back every day if we have to."

Mamapapa Dandel was suddenly struck with a new fear. "What if the gollogeens are cold too? Oh dear! I hadn't thought of that!"

"Please Mam," said Evie. "We have to stay and help find them."

"I'm really sorry, Evie. It's too late, too dark and too cold. Even if we stay to look for them, we won't see them in this light. We will have to go home." Evie was growing too cold to protest.

"We'll be back tomorrow, Mamapapa Dandel. Promise!"

"I can't feel my toes," said Jake. "They're going to fall off, aren't they?!"

"Don't be silly, Jake," said Evie. "Why would they fall off?"

"It was on that programme. Frostbite can make your toes fall off. They even showed this black and wrinkly toe that fell off someone. It's true!"

"Well, we'll be back at the car soon, so I think you'll be okay," said Evie. "I'm more worried about Daffi and Bretia and Monty. What if they are out there all shivering and lonely and cold? Mam, what's that word for when you get too cold? Hypo-something." But as soon as she said it and saw the look on Mam's face, she realised that it might be best not to say anything in front of Mamapapa Dandel.

Just then, Chaser suddenly started barking and pawing at the bottom of the bank. He pulled on the lead, trying to drag Mam up it.

"Down, Chaser! Down!" Mam cried and then whoosh! The lead slipped from her grasp as Chaser pulled himself with all his might up the bank.

"Oh no!" Mam watched helplessly as Chaser hopped easily up the steep slope on his four legs. A few metres up he suddenly stopped behind a tree growing out of the bank and started pawing the ground, barking. Evie tried to follow him.

"No, Evie!" cried Mam. "It's too steep!"

"But what if it's them, Mam?!"

"No! It's no good rescuing anyone if you get into danger yourself!"

Chaser lay down on the ground. What had he found?

They did not have to wait long to find out. The next minute Chaser walked very carefully back down the last couple of metres of the bank. Sitting on his back were Bretia and Monty, and held very carefully in his mouth was a terrified Daffi. He bent his head low and gently placed Daffi on the ground at Evie's feet.

"Daffi!" said Evie. But Daffi did not say anything. She was breathing gently but looked very cold and very shocked.

"Bretia! Monty! I'm so happy to see you!" Trying to be extra gentle, Evie stroked the fur on Daffi's back with her little finger. "What happened?" Mamapapa Dandel came over and started licking Daffi all over. Daffi was too big for Dandel's pouch, but she huddled her body next to Daffi and told Bretia and Monty to do the same. They formed a warm blanket around Daffi.

Evie stood back then and together with Jake and Mam looked on at the group of gollogans. Chaser sat next to them as if to guard them all.

Mam squatted down and pulled off her hat.

"Here," she said. "How about you hop into my hat and I'll carry you all to the car."

"To the car?" asked Mamapapa Dandel suspiciously.

"Yes," said Mam. "Daffi needs a vet.

Someone who looks after sick animals," Mam explained.

Daffi was still breathing weakly and had her eyes closed. It looked like she had bumped her head in the fall as there was a large lump developing near her left eye and one of her arms looked like it was in a very strange position.

"But Amaranthine ..."

Mam interrupted Dandel, "I know, I know. Amaranthine would not agree to it. Amaranthine is your healer, I understand that, but believe me, this time, Daffi needs a vet."

Evie remembered that Amaranthine trusted time and the healing power of plants and flowers. And in turn, all the gollogans trusted Amaranthine, because more often than not her potions and lotions worked. Indigo had explained to Evie that

Amaranthine was also fond of the old saying "time heals all wounds", so the gollogans were never quite sure if it was her herbal remedies or the passing of time that cured them. Amaranthine would have said both because the herbal medicines only worked slowly over time, as the body was slowly changed by the herbs. Amaranthine's other favourite expression was "the cure is in the care." And they all knew exactly what that meant. Just knowing that Amaranthine was looking after them, giving them love and attention, allowed them to rest and in most cases give their bodies a chance to heal.

But even Mam knew that Amaranthine could do little to heal broken bones and bumped heads — she had seen Gurrem's limp for herself the very first night they had spotted the gollogans near the tower. Back at the house Indigo had explained his fall from the branch, his broken leg and how it had healed awkwardly.

Evie could see now that Mamapapa Dandel was very unsure of this plan, but she was also very worried about Daffi.

"The cure is in the care," she said to Mamapapa Dandel, remembering Indigo's words, "and Mamapapa Dandel, please don't worry, we are going to take care of Daffi."

On hearing this familiar gollogan phrase, Mamapapa Dandel relaxed.

"Okay then." With that, she hopped into the hat. Bretia and Monty followed her, then Mam gently picked up Daffi and placed her next to them, so they could continue their job as a gollogan blanket.

Jake walked Chaser back to the car while Mam cradled the gollogans in her arms. Usually Chaser would be nearly pulling Jake over on the lead, but this time Chaser was

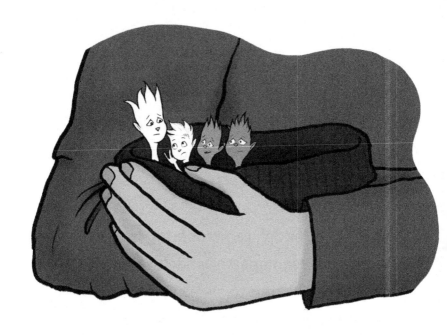

keeping close to his precious find and staying right by everyone's side.

The cardboard recycling box was in the boot of the car. Mam lined it with Jake's jumper found lying on the floor of the car and nestled the red hat in on top of it with its cargo of four small gollogans. Chaser hopped in beside them and just lay there panting. Everyone could tell he was not going to touch the gollogans. Strangely, he was now less of a chaser and more of a protector. The gollogans were clearly like family to him.

On the journey, Evie, Jake and Mam were all silent. They did not know it, but the same worried thoughts were running through all their minds. What would the vet make of the gollogans? And would she be able to help?

Chapter Eight
The First Vet

Getting the gollogans past the receptionist was easy. She had thought they wanted an appointment for Chaser so had said nothing. It was only when they went into the vet's treatment room and Mam placed the red hat on the examination table that things took a strange turn.

From inside the hat, Daffi was starting to come around and could hear everything that was going on, but she wasn't able to

move or see much outside the hat. She could
sense Mamapapa Dandel, Monty and Bretia
breathing fast beside her.

"Lift him up there for me," the vet said
as she turned to get her supplies ready. Daffi
saw the confused look on the vet's face as she
turned back and stared at the hat.

"She can't see us!" Daffi heard Mamapapa
Dandel whisper. "She can only see a red
woolly hat!"

The puzzled vet asked again. "Please lift
Chaser onto the table for me."

Evie's mam looked at the hat in
confusion. Outside the window the light
was fading fast.

"Oh!" Mam exclaimed. "I'm not here
for Chaser, I'm here for …." Mam paused
and Evie spoke instead: "Could we maybe
switch off the lights?" But the vet ignored
Evie.

"Please, if we switch off the lights you will see what we mean," said Mam.

Inside the hat, to her dismay, Daffi could hear the worried whispers of the other gollogans.

"Are you sure she's friendly?" said Bretia.

"She's a giant," said Mamapapa Dandel, her tail starting to flick rapidly. "We can't be sure — and whatever Evie's mam does now, we are all about to be seen!"

Daffi watched with one sleepy eye as Mamapapa Dandel crept to the edge of the hat, whispering loudly. "Follow me, gollogeens!" And with that, Mamapapa Dandel, Bretia, and Monty all took a flying leap from the hat to another part of the room. *What about me?* Thought Daffi, suddenly scared. *They forgot about me!* Daffi's fur, which had been flickering with cold, was now flickering more strongly in fear, as the vet walked over to switch off the light. Daffi tried to move, but it was no use. Her paws were so heavy and sleepy.

Darkness fell over the room. Outside, the glow of the sunset had fully disappeared. And the hat still looked empty.

"Wait!" Daffi heard Evie's mam say. There were sounds of fumbling, then suddenly the glow of a giant's phone. The torchlight was beamed towards the ceiling. The vet turned back to look into the hat and her eyes locked with Daffi's. Daffi looked away towards Evie who was staring over at her mam, confused and scared. *They must be wondering where the others are,* Daffi thought.

"Behind you!" Daffi tried to say, but her tongue would not move properly. But it was okay, Evie was turning to look behind her. She must have heard them. The vet followed

Evie's gaze, then appearing shocked and confused, turned to look back at Daffi.

"Can you see them?" asked Mam, anxiously.

"Erm ..." The vet was pale. "Erm, yes. I can see them. Yes." Daffi watched as the vet nervously stroked a strand of hair back behind her ear and pushed her glasses up

her nose. Even though she smelt strongly of grasses and flowers, her scent still hit the back of Daffi's throat sharply. It was not like the wildflowers in the woodland.

"Yes," said the vet again. "But what is it? I mean, what are they?" she said looking over at the chair.

"They're gollogans," explained Mam. "You know, from Carrickgollogan up the road."

"Wow! Well, I mean, of course," said the vet, recovering from her shock and trying to sound professional again.

"It's okay," said Evie. "They don't bite. But we're worried that Daffi is a bit too cold. What's the word for that, hypofarmer?" Daffi knew how much Evie loved the taste of long words on her tongue.

"Hypothermia," said the vet smiling.

"I couldn't believe it when I saw them myself," said Mam.

The vet relaxed a little more, "I mean, well, I'll be honest with you, I heard about gollogans when I was little, but I didn't know they really existed. I thought they were a fairy-tale, like leprechauns or gnomes or well, fairies!" She laughed a little, still clearly nervous.

The vet seemed friendlier now, calmer, Daffi thought. Just as well, because she was looking down at her again. "That's a nasty bump she has on her forehead. Let me have a look at that."

"Ow!" Daffi winced as the vet shone a searing light into her eyes.

"Well, there are no signs of concussion. What happened to, er, this gollogan?" the vet asked.

"Her name's Daffi," said Evie.

"What a lovely name," said the vet. "Can you tell me what happened to Daffi, er..."

"Evie. My name's Evie."

"And I'm Orla," said the vet. "Nice to meet you, Evie. Can you tell me what happened to Daffi, Evie?"

So she *is* friendly, thought Daffi, relieved.

"She fell down the steep slope in Knocksink," said Jake.

"I see," said the vet. "I'll just check her over."

At the sight of the vet's hands coming down towards her, Daffi fainted back into sleep.

Orla very carefully lifted Daffi out of the hat and then gently felt her arms and legs to check for broken bones.

"A dislocated shoulder," Evie heard the vet muttering to herself. There was a loud "pop" as the vet clicked Daffi's arm back into its socket. Daffi stirred a little, but soon fell back into a daze. Orla continued. "No bones broken, it seems. And luckily, no concussion either. I think the best cure for this little one is a good rest and plenty of love and attention."

Over on the chair, Mamapapa Dandel was suddenly very agitated. Mamapapa Dandel had not seen the vet fix Daffi's dislocated shoulder and she was very annoyed. Hearing the sound of Mamapapa Dandel's tail flicking against the back of the chair, Evie turned around to look at her. Mamapapa Dandel looked about ready to explode into flames with anger.

"You mean," she said to Evie, growing as loud as a gollogan can, which is not very loud at all. "You mean, that your mam brought us all this way in that jolting and juddering boulder-wagon to a giant healer, or vet or whatever you call them and she has nothing better to say than what Amaranthine would say herself? And now we have been seen!"

"Ssh! Mamapapa Dandel," said Bretia. "She's still helping her!"

"But," said the vet continuing. "She has been suffering from quite severe hypothermia, so I am going to inject some warmed water to bring her body temperature back up." She turned to prepare what she needed on the counter behind her and soon brought out a small syringe filled with warmed water.

"No!" cried Evie, horrified at the sight of the needle.

"It's okay, Evie," said Mam. "It's to help her recover."

"I can't look!" Evie ran over to Mam and hid her head under Mam's scarf. Evie could not stand the sight of needles. Jake did not mind. Usually Evie was the one telling *him* not to be a scaredy-cat, but when it came to needles it was the other way around. Now, Jake got to feel like the big brother for once.

Orla was just lowering the needle down to Daffi when suddenly there was a BOOM! Clatter! *Splash*!

Mamapapa Dandel had landed right on top of the syringe, knocking it out of Orla's hand and scattering drops of water all over the hat and all over Daffi. At that very moment another vet walked into the room.

Chapter Nine
The Second Vet

Mamapapa Dandel froze. The dim lighting had made the room look like it was not being used. For the second vet, it was the quickest way to the reception.

"Oh, sorry!" The new vet was an older man with greying hair, his face falling gently off his bones and wrinkling as it went. Tight wrinkles around his mouth suggested that he was used to pressing his lips together in disapproval. He was business-like and quick

in his movements and his presence only added to the mounting tension in the room. He glanced at the examination table to see which animal he had disturbed. "Oh!" he said again. "Oh, now!" Never in his thirty years of veterinary practice had he ever come across such a creature before.

Mam tried to swipe the phone screen so she could switch the torchlight off, but it would not work for some reason and then in a fluster she dropped her phone. Declan, the second vet, got a long view of dozy

Daffi, now looking quite vulnerable on the enormous metal examination table. Near Daffi, Mamapapa Dandel stood staring up at him, unable to move with fright.

While everyone was distracted by this new development, Orla swiftly injected the remaining warm salt-water solution into Daffi.

The new vet was suspicious now. That was no ordinary hamster, guinea pig, rabbit, rat, mouse or well, even squirrel, not that people usually kept squirrels as pets. It looked strangely human. It couldn't be a, *what were they called again?* His Uncle Ger had told him about them as a child. *No, put that silly thought out of your head* he thought to himself. *You're a grown man.*

"What is that rodent on your examination table, Orla?" He suddenly spotted Bretia and Monty on the chair. *Were they all over the building? An infestation? Maybe he ought to call pest-control.*

"Declan! Erm, it's, um..." Orla fumbled for words for the second time that afternoon.

Evie untangled herself from Mam's scarf and Mam bent down to pick up her phone, switching off the light. The whole room was plunged into darkness.

"What the devil?" Declan quickly flicked on the main light. "What the —?" The creatures had all vanished! Either he needed to ring pest-control or he needed to turn this new species over to the authorities for investigation. They would want to take photographs, study them, maybe even breed some of them in the zoo? Maybe they were in danger of extinction? It was his job to make sure things were done properly. You could not have these, oh, what were they called again? Didn't it begin with a "g"? Goolagans?

Gollygoons? Galligans? Anyway, you could not have them in the surgery and not tell people. What was Orla thinking, not telling him straight away? Declan would not admit it to himself, but he was not just upholding the rules, he was also the tiniest bit jealous that Orla, his junior, had been the first to see them.

"Orla," he said. "Don't leave this room! I'll get a hamster box. We need to find them." He went carefully back out the side door, closing it quickly behind him.

"Mam!" cried Evie in horror. "What's he going to do with them?"

"Quick!" said Orla. "You'd better go!"

Mam grabbed the hat with a still drowsy Daffi inside. Mamapapa Dandel ran over and hopped in next to her. Mam popped the hat on the chair for Bretia and Monty to climb in. Then, Evie carefully picked up the hat while Mam took Chaser who had started barking and pawing at the door that Declan had disappeared through. Evie clutched the hat in her hand and the whole Quinn family quickly made their way out to reception, just as Declan was hot-footing his way through it with the hamster box. The receptionist was on the phone.

"Orla told us to go. The gollogans are ..." Mam, not wanting to lie, waved vaguely towards the consulting room, still moving towards the door. "Okay," said Declan. "We'll keep you posted."

"Okay," said Mam, relieved. As Declan went back into the consulting room, she hustled Evie and Jake quickly out of the door of the surgery. The receptionist put the phone down. "Er, Mrs Quinn! Did you want to settle up before you go or will I —?!"

But there was no time to stop and pay. Their car was parked right outside the window of the surgery and they carefully placed the hat back into the cardboard box.

"This is like a gangster movie!" said Jake excitedly, as they all rushed to get into the car. "It's like we're criminals running from the scene of the crime!"

Mam reversed out of the car park and accelerated up the road, the engine revving loudly like a formula one car.

"Wow, Evie!" said Jake. "This is so cool!" Evie nodded, wide-eyed with excitement and terror.

They were on the run.

Chapter Ten
The Return

Mam drove as fast as speed limits allowed straight back to Knocksink. It was time to get Daffi home again. The best medicine for her now was a good winter sleep and even with the best will in the world only the gollogans could give her that.

Evie reluctantly had to say goodbye again to her gollogan friends. They all crossed the bridge together and then to avoid disturbing the sleeping gollogans in

the crevice said their goodbyes there. Daffi
had by now woken up fully. Her head was
a bit sore, but she said she felt otherwise
okay, just tired and well ready for the
long winter sleep. Monty and Bretia were
relieved to hear Daffi talking again. They
stayed close by her side as they made their
way back to the crevice.

Evie watched as the gollogans slowly
walked away, then with Jake and Mam, she
turned and crossed back over the bridge.

"Mam," she said, "I'm sad."

"Me, too," said Mam unexpectedly.

"Me, three," said Jake.

"We'll be missing them again," said Mam.
"They certainly keep us busy!"

Evie smiled a little. She could not wait
for spring! What was it Daffi and Indigo had
said before? Come when they see the first
primrose? She had printed out a big picture

of a primrose and stuck it up on her bedroom wall. She had wanted to be absolutely sure that she did not look for the wrong flower.

"Will that vet find them?" asked Jake.

"No, not at all. Sure, he didn't see which way our car went, did he?"

"I suppose not," said Jake.

They all set off back to the car, warm cups of hot milk beckoning to them from home. Chaser paused and let out a howl to the trees which echoed around the woodland

and voiced all their sad feelings in a kind of gollogan salute.

Meanwhile, Mamapapa Dandel, Daffi, Monty and Bretia were surprised to discover that not a single gollogan was asleep. What was going on? And then they heard it. A cry! A tiny new-born gollogan was cradled in Mamapapa Nettie's pouch.

"What's her name?" asked Bretia.

Nettie looked up from her beautiful little bundle. "Amethyst," she replied.

"Oh, so she's ..."

"Yes," replied Nettie. "She was meant to be born in spring-time, but came just a little early. She's a purple gollogan."

"Like Baby Violet then," said Monty.

"Yes," said Nettie.

"But I didn't think you could have two purples in one generation," said Daffi.

"You are right, Daffi," said Amaranthine coming up behind them. "It is a bad omen, a bad omen indeed. But come now, you must rest. Here is some comfrey for that cut on your head." Amaranthine gently applied a smelly paste to Daffi's scalp.

"Oh, Amaranthine," said Mamapapa Dandel. "Don't be saying that as if it is wisdom. We all know that is an old gollogan's tale. All gollogeens are a blessing." She winked affectionately at Daffi. "Or I should say, all gollogeens are a blessing, especially when they're not messing!" Mamapapa Dandel's mood had brightened considerably since arriving back at the tunnel. At first she had been cross with Daffi for all the trouble she had caused, but now she was clearly just relieved to have her back safe and sound. And now, with the unexpected arrival of the new baby and all the other gollogans awake on their arrival back, it felt like autumn festival all over again.

But Amaranthine did not like Mamapapa Dandel challenging her in this way. She was not used to it. Amaranthine could feel the energies of the clan shifting, not only in the way Dandel spoke to her, but in this baby being born early, as a purple. It was surely for a reason! And until she could figure out why she could not rest. But before then, there were other important matters to deal with. Three of the clan had tried to leave and this was another sign of the shifting sands all around her: The move to Knocksink, the new baby, the gollogeens running off, so many unexpected changes. And at their usual time of sleep!

"So, you three, do you want to tell me why you all set off on this unwise adventure?"

Daffi knew better than to make up a story for Amaranthine. The power of her piercing gaze could scythe any tall tale down to size.

"It was my idea," she admitted. "I kind of thought it would be fun. To be a human pet or something. And," she almost whispered it, "to not live by gollogan rules anymore."

Amaranthine started on hearing this admission. To not live by rules! How she had so longed for that herself as a gollogeen!

"But, dear Daffi," she said. "You may choose not to live by our rules if you wish, but you can never escape the laws of nature. We all must live by those. Cold weather rules that we must stay in the warm or dress warmly for fear of freezing our bodies; a steep slope rules that we must go down it carefully, with due respect for the possibility of our falling and injuring ourselves; a lack of food in the winter-time rules that we must sleep and not be running around using up our energy. But, I suspect, you have learnt all this now for yourself. We might want to change nature, but it never really goes away. Everything we do affects everything and everyone else for good or for ill. That is our choice. But we have to live with the consequences of that choice. I trust you will choose more wisely, next time, Daffi? And you too, Monty and Bretia?"

The three gollogeens nodded.

"And now, as a consequence of all this excitement, I am profoundly tired," said Amaranthine. Her voice wavered at the end and she found herself dizzily sinking down to the ground.

"Amaranthine?" said Daffi.

But Amaranthine was already far away in a blissful gollogan slumber.

"Daffi, let's play with the new baby," called Bretia, who had already gone over to Mamapapa Nettie.

Daffi started to head over then stopped herself.

"It's winter, Bretia. Time to sleep."

And before long, Daffi and all the gollogans were calmly and restfully snoring.

The Gollogans in Winter

In this second book of the Gollogans series, young gollogan Daffi is fed up with her woodland life and convinces her friends Monty and Bretia to find a "giant" house to live in. But can they survive on their own in the wild? And what if all the giants are not as friendly as Evie and Jake?

Helen O'Sullivan is a word-lover. When not writing books, reading books, teaching or learning new languages, she can be found attempting to sew, knit and do gymnastics (not all at once), selling eggs, growing vegetables, cuddling chickens, petting dogs and getting out into the wild with her own three young woodland explorers.

David Hallangen has been drawing a variety of entertaining yet informative nonsense since 1998, a career spanning two millennia and three haircuts. He currently works from his gloriously cluttered home studio, with his family and remaining marbles.

WOODSORREL PRESS

www.helenosullivan.ie
Instagram: @helenosullivan_author

For teaching resources and activities related to the Gollogans series, please visit the website at www.helenosullivan.ie or contact riverrunreadingroom@gmail.com

Printed in Great Britain
by Amazon

35137749R00081